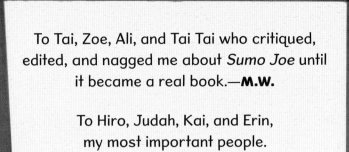

To Tai, Zoe, Ali, and Tai Tai who critiqued, edited, and nagged me about *Sumo Joe* until it became a real book.—**M.W.**

To Hiro, Judah, Kai, and Erin, my most important people. *Pax familia!*—**N.I.**

AUTHOR'S SOURCES

"About Aikido." United States Aikido Federation. Accessed June 6, 2016. http://www.usaikifed.com/about/aikido/.

Gutman, Bill. *Sumo Wrestling*. Minneapolis, MN: Capstone Press, 1995.

Hall, Mina. *The Big Book of Sumo*. Berkeley, CA: Stone Bridge Press, 1997.

Long, Walter. *Sumo: A Pocket Guide*. Rutland, VT: Charles E. Tuttle Company, 1989.

Lynch, William. "Sumo Wrestling Techniques and Training Routines." Livestrong. September 11, 2017. https://www.livestrong.com/article/479298-sumo-wrestling-techniquesand-training-routines.

Murphy, Jennifer. "Basic Principles of Aikido Help Turn an Attack Into Opportunity." *The Wall Street Journal*, November 30, 2015. https://www.wsj.com/articles/basic-principles-of-aikido-help-one-turn-an-attack-into-opportunity-1448899850.

"What is Aikido?" Midwest Aikido Center. Accessed June 6, 2016. http://www.midwestaikidocenter.org/what-aikido.

Text copyright © 2019 by Mia Wenjen | Illustrations copyright © 2019 by Nat Iwata
All rights reserved. No part of this book may be reproduced, transmitted, or stored in an information retrieval system in any form or by any means, electronic, mechanical, photocopying, recording, or otherwise, without written permission from the publisher.
LEE & LOW BOOKS Inc., 95 Madison Avenue, New York, NY 10016 | leeandlow.com
Edited by Kandace Coston | Designed by Abby Dening
Production by The Kids at Our House | The text is set in Sweater School Regular
The illustrations are rendered digitally | Manufactured in China by Toppan
Printed on paper from responsible resources
10 9 8 7 6 5 4 3 2 1
First Edition

LIBRARY OF CONGRESS CATALOGING-IN-PUBLICATION DATA
Names: Wenjen, Mia, author. | Iwata, Nat, illustrator.
Title: Sumo Joe / by Mia Wenjen; illustrated by Nat Iwata.
Description: First edition. | New York: Lee & Low Books Inc., [2019] |
Summary: "Sumo Joe and his friends pretend to be sumo wrestlers, but when his little sister, who takes aikido, wants to join them, Sumo Joe must choose between his friends and his sister. Includes author's note about sumo and aikido, and illustrated glossary"—Provided by publisher.
Identifiers: LCCN 2018042635 | ISBN 9781620148020 (hardcover: alk. paper)
Subjects: | CYAC: Stories in rhyme. | Sumo—Fiction. | Aikido—Fiction. |
Wrestling—Fiction. Classification: LCC PZ8.3.W46525 Su 2019 | DDC [E]—dc23
LC record available at https://lccn.loc.gov/2018042635

SUMO JOE

BY **Mia Wenjen**   ILLUSTRATED BY **Nat Iwata**

LEE & LOW BOOKS INC.
New York

Get up early,
have to hurry,

Sumo Joe.

Strong big bro,
built for sumo,

gentle, though.

Build the ring,
here we go,

practice **sumo**!

Special belt,
wrapped like so,

takes a duo.

Mawashi long,
knotted strong,

time for sumo.

Hands on knees,
leg raised slow,

practice **shiko**.

Stomping strong,
demons be gone,

it's from **Shinto**.

Slide hands and feet,
avoid defeat,

drill called **teppo**.

Sacred salt fling,
to bless the ring,

at the **dohyō**.

Lift thigh high,
twist belt low,

uchimuso!

Who is here
with no fear?

AIKIDO JO!

She wants to join boy-only place.

She's not allowed
in sacred space.

She wants to prove
that she's got moves. . . .

Step in, step back,
time to attack,

SUMO JOE.

Circle the ring,
stay down low,

AIKIDO JO.

Step out of ring
with heel or toe,

lose sumo.

Don't move a thing!
Sidestep! Fling!

Bye-bye, Joe!

Aikido Jo beats Sumo Joe!

KIYAH!

AUTHOR'S NOTE

Sumo Joe and his friends re-create the traditions of sumo wrestling in their own way. They tie on scarves for their belts (*mawashi*) and build a ring (*dohyō*) made of pillows. They perform *shiko*, a stomping exercise used to drive away evil spirits, and begin their matches by throwing salt to purify the ring. All these practices are based on rituals of sumo wrestling rooted in Shinto traditions.

During a sumo match, two wrestlers use a variety of techniques that include pushing, shoving, slapping, throwing, tripping, and grappling to knock each other down or out of the ring. Although it seems as if the bigger wrestler would always win, this is not the case. Like Sumo Joe and his friends, sumo wrestlers come in different shapes and sizes. It takes a combination of strategy, agility, and technique to win a match.

Aikido Jo uses her training in aikido to compete against her older brother, Sumo Joe. Like a matador in a bullring, aikido martial artists use graceful and precise movements to redirect their attacker's energy and throw the person off balance. Aikido does not have competitions, so it's only for fun that Aikido Jo would square off against Sumo Joe in a match.

Sumo has traditionally been considered a sport for men, though there have been instances during the long evolution of sumo that included women competing in the ring. Women are not allowed to touch the dohyō after it has been purified with salt, which is why Sumo Joe's friends try to keep Aikido Jo from entering their ring. In recent years, however, there has been a surge of interest and support for women in sumo wrestling, prompting calls for the sport to be more inclusive.

GLOSSARY

Aikido is a modern Japanese martial art developed by Morihei Ueshiba. It's a form of self-defense that protects both the attacker and defender from injury. Because aikido redirects the attacker's energy, it can be very effective even if the defender is much smaller than the opponent.

Mawashi is the belt sumo wrestlers wear during training and competitions. It measures about 30 feet (9 meters) in length and is made from cotton or silk. The mawashi gets wrapped several times around the sumo wrestler in a precise way so that it fits securely against the wrestler's body. Then it is tied in the back with a large knot.

Shiko is one of the basic sumo stomping exercises used to build leg strength. Sumo wrestlers slowly raise one leg high to the side in the air, then bring it down with great force in a stomping motion. Wrestlers perform shiko in the dohyō ceremoniously to drive away bad spirits.

Dohyō is the ring where sumo bouts are held. It is about 15 feet (4.6 meters) in diameter and is made of rice-straw bales mounted on a square platform. The entire surface is covered in sand, which helps the judges determine whether or not a wrestler touched the ground outside of the ring.

Figure A

Figure B

Shinto is an ancient Japanese religious system. It connects present-day Japan with its past by honoring *kami*, which is the spirit or energy of all things both living and dead, including people, plants, and animals.

Sumo is a competitive, full-contact wrestling sport from Japan. Sumo can be traced back to ancient Shinto rituals that were practiced to ensure a bountiful harvest and to honor the spirits. Sumo wrestlers also served as warriors to warlords during the age of the samurai. Its present-day form developed during the Edo period (1603–1868), when the money raised from matches was used primarily to build shrines and temples. Today sumo in Japan is enjoyed by many people through six major tournaments a year.

Teppo is an exercise that helps strengthen a wrestler's arms and shoulders. The wrestler starts in a squat position, then reaches out to strike either a large wooden pole (also known as a teppo) or a partner with the palm of the right hand while simultaneously sliding the right foot forward. The wrestler then repeats the action, alternating between the left and right hands and feet.

Uchimuso is one of the eighty-two techniques that can be used to win a sumo match. In this particular technique, the sumo wrestler grips the opponent's belt with one hand and pulls down while simultaneously using the other hand to lift up the opponent's inner thigh, thus twisting the person off balance.